Squirrel!
A Maple's Busy Morning Adventure

By
Linda Bassick and Greg Rothwell

Illustrated by
Jackson Tupper

BURLINGTON, VERMONT

Copyright © 2020 by Linda Bassick & Greg Rothwell // Illustrations Copyright © 2024 by Jackson Tupper

All rights reserved. No part of this publication may be reproduced, distributed, or transmitted in any form or by any means, including photocopying, recording, or other electronic or mechanical methods, without the prior written permission of the publisher, except in the case of brief quotations embodied in critical reviews and certain other noncommercial uses permitted by copyright law.

Onion River Press
Burlington, VT
www.onionriverpress.com
info@onionriverpress.com

ISBN: 978-1-957184-48-7 // Library of Congress Control Number: 2024908345

This book is based on the song "Squirrel In A Tree" from the album "Maple's Busy Morning" by the Busy Morning Band.

Listen to "Squirrel In A Tree"

Scan the code to hop, swim, fly and listen along!

Have you ever tried to be a squirrel in a tree leaping from branch to branch?

**Have you ever tried to be a squirrel in a tree?
You could try it when you get the chance!**

**Have you ever tried to be a squirrel in a tree?
Snuggle down in your nest of leaves.**

**Have you ever tried to be a squirrel in a tree?
You can do it now if you please!**

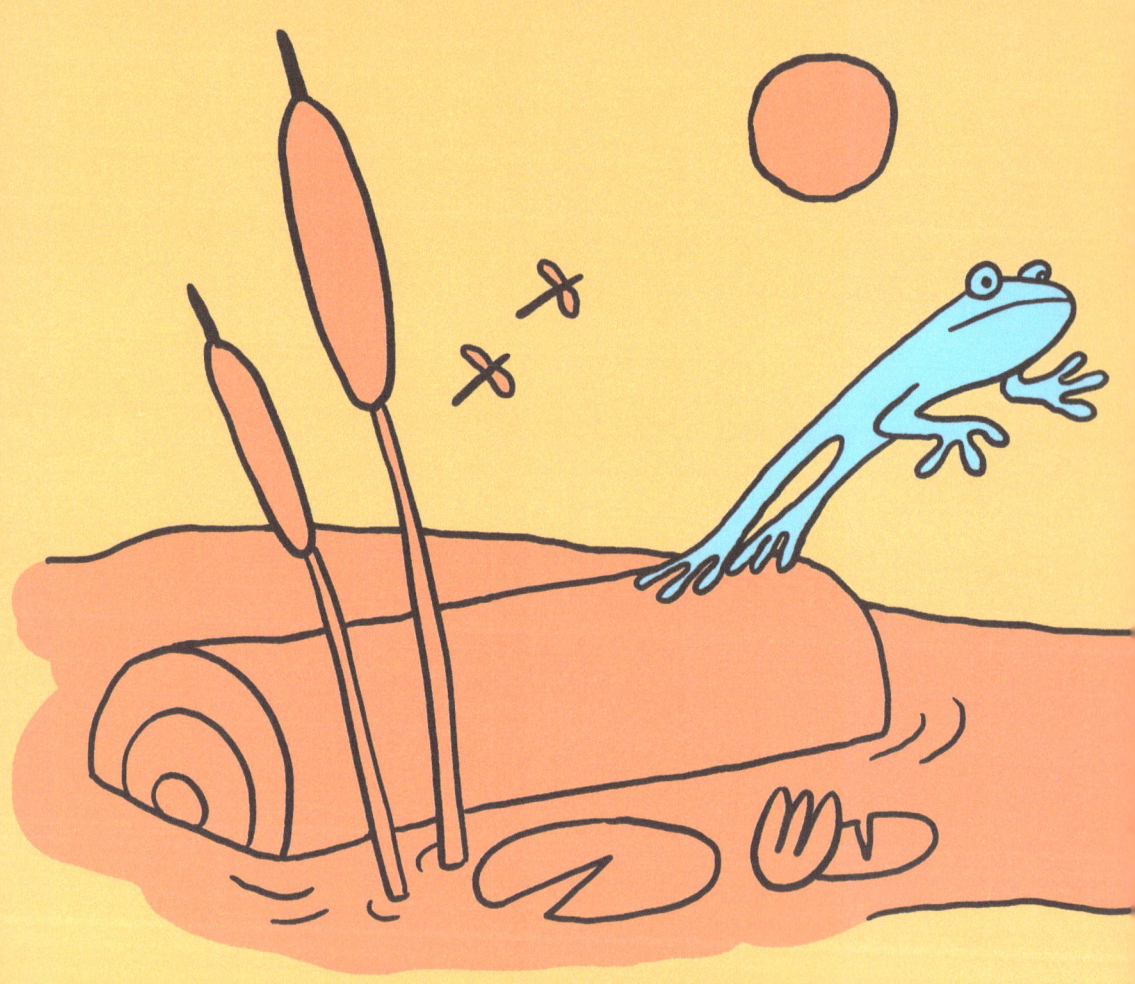

Down in the bog there are a bunch of logs where the sun is shining bright.

**Jump like a frog.
Jump from log to log.
Jump in the warm sunlight.**

**Over on a stone a turtle rests alone
warming their shell in the sun.**

The turtle isn't fazed when the frogs start to play, jumping over them for fun.

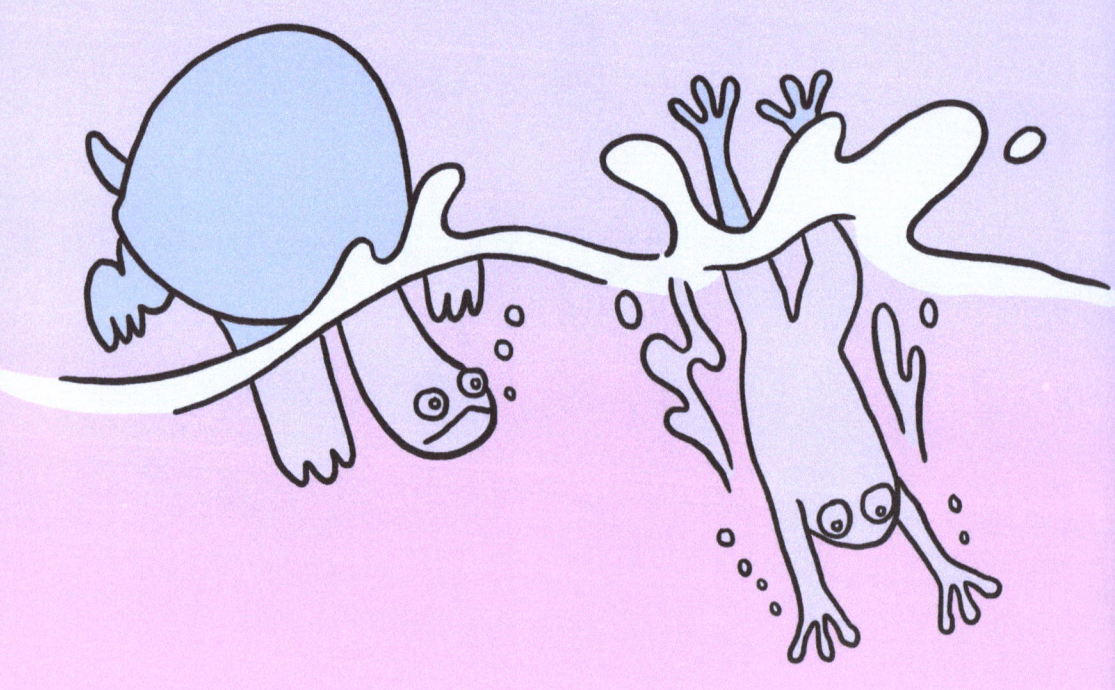

**Splash!
Jump into the water!
Feel the cool of the pool on your sunbaked skin.**

**The fish are so happy to see us!
It's like a pool party when we jump in.**

A duck paddles by with an eye on the sky ready to stretch their wings.

**They wave their wings goodbye and take off to fly.
"Quack, quack, quack," they sing.**

ICK QUACK

It feels so nice to fly so high up in the sky after that lovely rest.

They flew all around then landed on the ground and waddled off to their nest.

Were you a squirrel in a tree?
Were you a frog on a log?

**Were you a turtle on a stone resting all alone?
Were you a fish in the pool having fun at the party?**

Were you a duck in the sky

flying all the way home?

Fly home, fly home, fly home, fly home.

Printed in the USA
CPSIA information can be obtained
at www.ICGtesting.com
CBHW041634060724
11010CB00068B/68